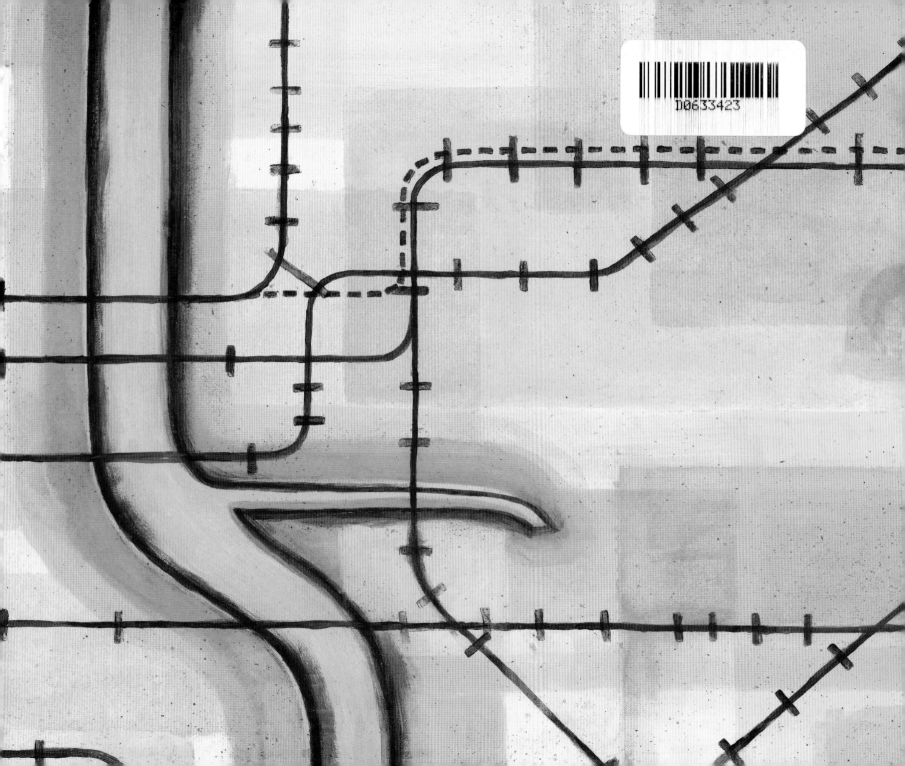

THIS IS A BORZOI BOOK PUBLISHED BY ALFRED A. KNOPF

Visit us on the Web! www.randomhouse.com/kids
Educators and librarians, for a variety of teaching tools,
visit us at www.randomhouse.com/teachers

Library of Congress Cataloging-in-Publication Data
Sarcone-Roach, Julia.
Subway story / Julia Sarcone-Roach.
p. cm.
Summary: Jessie, a subway car "born" in St. Louis, Missouri,
enjoys many years as an important part of the New York City
subway system, and after she is replaced by more modern cars,
she begins another important job.
Includes bibliographical references.
ISBN 978-0-375-85859-8 (trade) — ISBN 978-0-375-95859-5 (lib. bdg.) —
ISBN 978-0-375-98471-6 (ebook)
[1. Subways—New York (State)—New York—Fiction.
2. Artificial reefs—Fiction. 3. New York (N.Y.)—Fiction.] I. Title.
PZ7.S242Sub 2011
[E]—dc22
2010045487

The illustrations in this book were created using acrylic paint on paper.

Printed in the United States of America
October 2011
10 9 8 7 6 5 4 3 2
First Edition

To Cecile,
who first put Jessie on the tracks,
and to Nancy,
who brought her home

SUBWAY STORY

JULIA SARCONE-ROACH

ALFRED A. KNOPF  NEW YORK

When Jessie was born in St. Louis, Missouri,
she weighed 75,122 pounds and was 51½ feet long.

She had a loud horn, four big fans, four large windows,
bright lights for seeing, sturdy seats for sitting,
and a gleaming coat of paint.

She was a beautiful, shiny new subway car!

Jessie arrived at her new home
in New York City and
got to work right away.

She was strong and fast.
People relied on her to get to
their jobs or to school, or
to see their friends and family.

Jessie traveled all over the big, bustling city.

When the World's Fair began, Jessie had the special job of carrying visitors to the fairgrounds.

Sometimes Jessie helped carry unusual things.

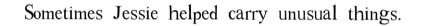

She made sure to go slower around the curves
so everyone—and everything—arrived safe.

Sometimes musicians practiced on board,
and Jessie was happy to provide some
rumbles and clickety-clacks
for their songs.

Even the occasional pigeon
came along for a ride.

No matter who or what was on board,
Jessie's favorite part of her route was the curve of the track
right before her tunnel ducked under the river.

She would speed up for the curve
and then zip down with a

SKREEET!

of sparks shooting off her wheels.

And even deep down under the river,
Jessie could hear the echoing

BaaaoOOM

of the tugboats far up above her.

If she passed another train, she'd always give a
friendly winK with a twinKle of her headlight.

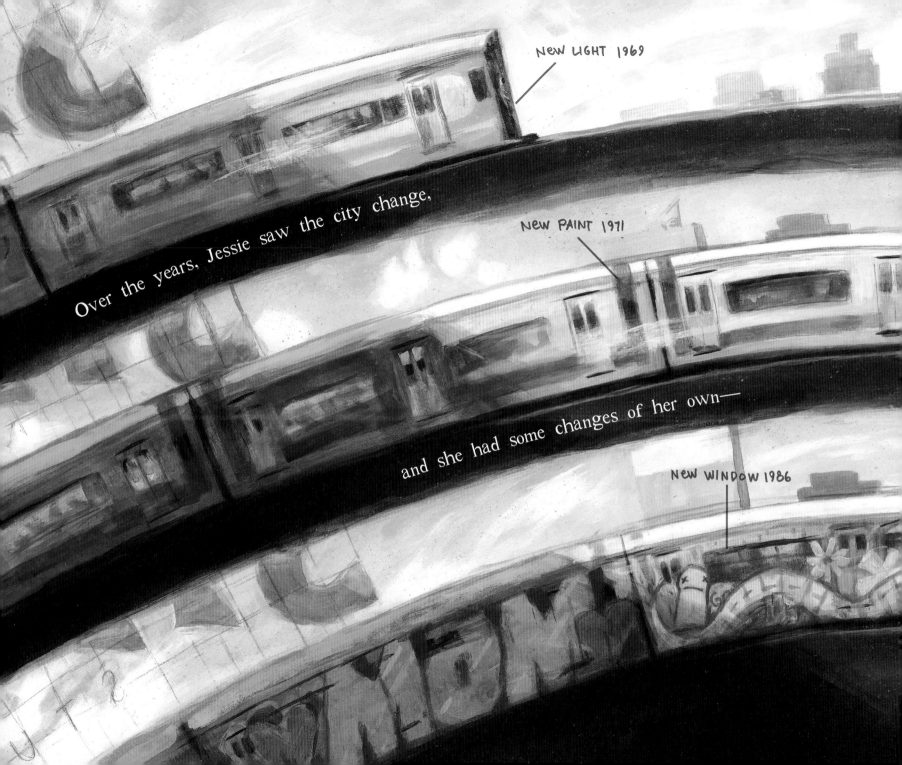

NEW LIGHT 1969

Over the years, Jessie saw the city change,

NEW PAINT 1971

and she had some changes of her own—

NEW WINDOW 1986

NEW DOOR 1978

her parts got fixed when they broke down,

LOTS OF NEW PAINT 1986

and she even got to change colors.

But when Jessie got older, a new coat of paint couldn't hide the cracks in her seats and the scratches and scuffs on her windows and floors.

By summer,
Jessie's fans were just not strong
enough to keep her passengers cool.
So newer, air-conditioned trains took over her route
during the summer months.

Jessie missed the people and the activity.

She was always glad when fall came
and she could go back to work.

Then one year the air turned frosty and the leaves changed color,
but nobody came to put Jessie back on her route.

She sat in a yard with the other older trains.

She thought about the people she had carried.
Did they notice that she was gone?

One day, workers came and moved Jessie inside. When they began removing her fans,
Jessie was excited. "Finally, I am getting fixed!" she thought.
As they pulled out her seats and windows,
Jessie began to feel much lighter.

But then she felt someone unbolting her doors.
"Wait!" she thought. "My doors aren't broken.
I need them!"

Instead of fixing her, the people were taking Jessie apart.
Off came her lights, her signs, her brakes, and her horn too!

Then they washed Jessie over and over again,
and left her with a group of other cleaned-up subway cars.

The cars were loaded onto a barge in the river,
and a tugboat pulled the barge out of the city harbor.
As the waves got bigger, Jessie felt the breezes
whistle through her empty windows.
Curious fish peered up at them
as the barge moved
into the open ocean.

"Will I ever get to see my city again?"
Jessie nervously thought.

After traveling for hours, the barge came to a stop.
The subway cars could see nothing but water.
Everything was quiet.

Suddenly the crane in the middle of the barge began to move.
It shoved the car next to Jessie to the edge of the barge.

SPLASH!!

The car went over and disappeared beneath the waves.
"Is that what will happen to me?" Jessie wondered.

And then she felt the crane beneath her, pushing her toward the edge.

Then—**whooosh!!**—Jessie plunged into the salty ocean.

Water thundered into every part
of Jessie, and it got
darker and darker

as she sank down,

down,

down,

until . . .

THUMP! She hit the ocean floor.
A huge cloud of sand and silt churned up around her,
and at first Jessie couldn't see anything.

Then out of the dimness came a little silver fish.
In and out of Jessie's windows and doors he swam. Soon there were more
curious little fish swirling around her. In the darkness, Jessie felt a little like
she was back in the subway tunnels she knew so well.

Over the next few days,
more fish decided to move in
and live with Jessie.

In the following weeks, shellfish settled inside
and plants began to grow all over her.

Then bigger fish from the deeper parts of the ocean
came to feed on the smaller fish.

Sometimes a dolphin or turtle
would stop by to visit.

Now Jessie lives on the ocean floor.

Tiny creatures called coral cling to the same poles
that people held on to when Jessie lived and worked aboveground.
Hundreds of fish dart through the doors that people once used.

Jessie was once an important part of the city where she lived.

And now a whole city
lives inside her.

AUTHOR'S NOTE

Jessie's story is inspired by a real subway car that arrived in New York for the 1964 World's Fair and was "reefed" off the coast of Delaware in 2001.

The car was a model R33 WF, which was one of the fleet of subway cars designed to impress and welcome visitors from around the world and to showcase the New York subway system. The first car of the model was even featured in TV ads and on a float in a parade.

After the World's Fair ended, the R33 WFs continued to work their routes. They began their lives on the tracks painted aquamarine and cream. Later on, like many other models of subway cars, the cars received the distinctive red paint job that gave them the nickname "Redbirds."

Throughout the world, people have found different ways to reuse older subway cars. In London, cars from the Underground have been made into artists' studios and work spaces. In China, subway cars have been converted into shelters for people who were left homeless by earthquakes. Museums, schools, and even restaurants have preserved or reused retired subway cars. Some countries are selling old cars to other railroad systems.

After they were taken out of service, many of the Redbirds were reused as artificial reefs in the Atlantic.

A reef is an underwater chain of rock or a sandbar. And just as a house is built up from a foundation, a reef is a base where undersea creatures can attach and build homes. People have been creating artificial reefs all over the world for thousands of years. Shipwrecks may have been some of the first accidental artificial reefs. Modern reef builders have also experimented with reused materials—concrete pipes, steel highway bridges, even planes, automobiles, trucks, tugboats—and subway cars.

After a subway car is sunk to the ocean floor, barnacles, blue mussels, oysters, soft corals, and sponges quickly begin to grow. Then sea bass, triggerfish, and flounder arrive. The flounder like to lie in the sand on the roof of the car, while the other fish live inside. Soon bigger fish from deeper in the ocean, like tuna and mackerel, come to eat the tiny fish that dart out of the waving sea grasses carpeting the floor of the car.

Though they are not as great or as long-lasting as natural reefs, the subway cars will provide homes to generations of underwater creatures and new fishing grounds for both people and fish.

For more information, visit:
epa.gov/reg3esd1/coast/reefs.htm
mta.info/mta/museum (for information on the New York Transit Museum)
nycsubway.org
reefball.org
www.fw.delaware.gov/Fisheries/Pages/ArtificialReefProgram.aspx

Bibliography:
Cooper, Martha, and Henry Chalfant. *Subway Art.* New York: Owl Books, Henry Holt and Company, 1984.
Hanley, Robert. "Subway Cars' Last Stop: Under Sea, Not Ground." *The New York Times,* July 4, 2003.
Roach, John. "Artificial Reefs Made with Sunken Subway Cars, Navy Ships." *National Geographic News,* August 18, 2006.
Sansone, Gene. *New York Subways: An Illustrated History of New York City's Transit Cars.* Centennial ed. Baltimore: Johns Hopkins University Press, 2004.
Urbina, Ian. "Growing Pains for a Deep-Sea Home Built of Subway Cars." *The New York Times,* April 8, 2008.

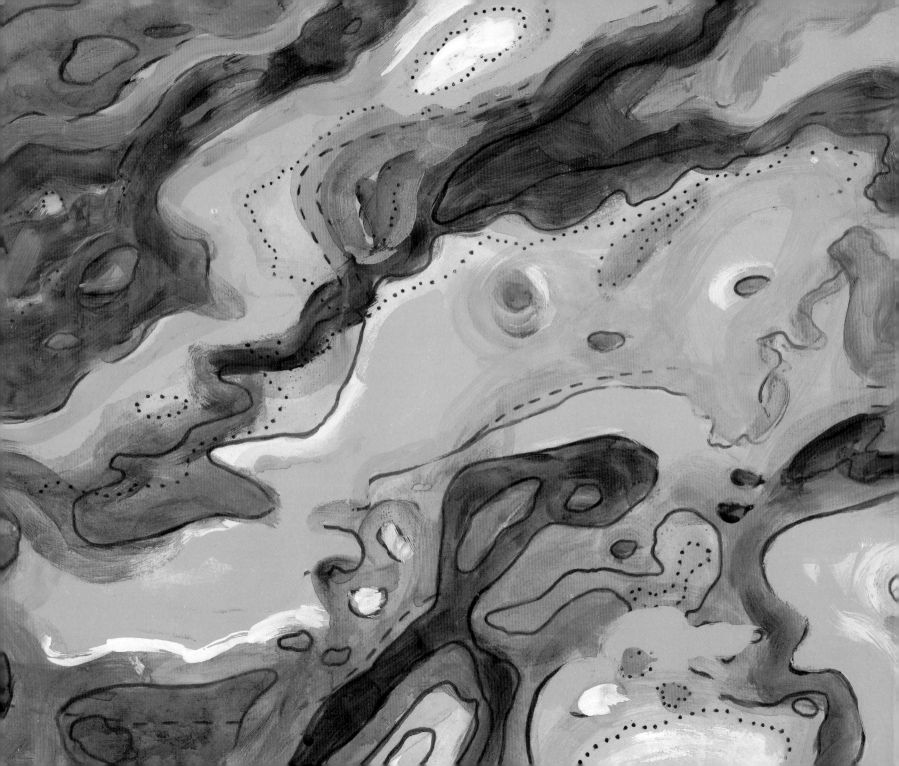